To Corey

We love you so
much!
Uncle Duke
+
Aunt ♡
Nancy
:)

DINO BUILDERS!

by Derek Alexandrenko

It's going to be another busy day in Dino Valley, the Dino Builders have a big job to do! Tommy Tyrannosaurus arrives with the bulldozer to clear the work site!

Stacey Stegosaurus pulls up in the concrete truck to pour the foundation. Vinney Velociraptor and his crew smooth out the fresh concrete with their power trowels.

The Dino Builders work together to get the tough job done!

Scotty Spinosaurus uses his powerful crane to lift the beams, while Benny Brachiosaurus welds the building framework.

Tammy and Theo Triceratops work hard
to get the windows and doors in place!

This Dino build is really starting to take shape!
Do you know what this building will be?

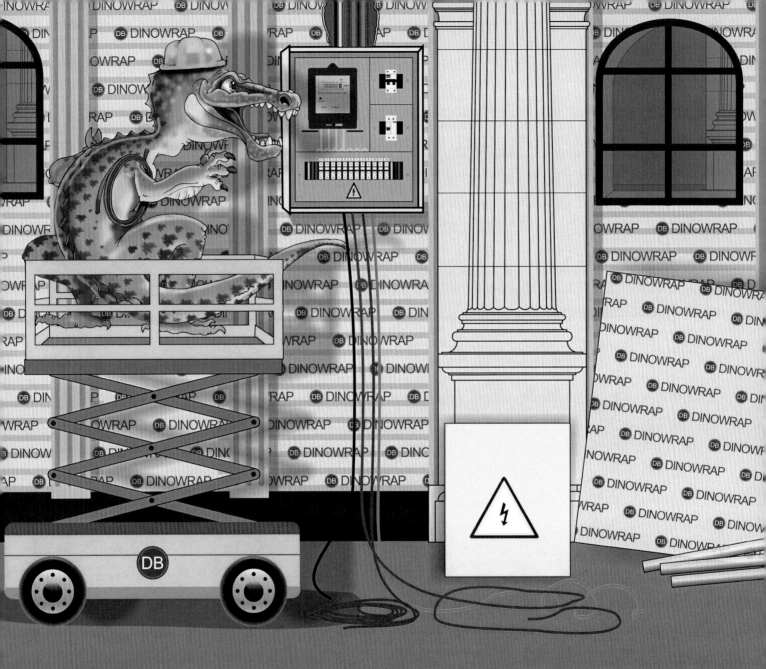

Billy Baryonyx and Patty Parasaurolophus work
hard to put in all the wires and pipes.

There is still so much to do!

Quentin Quetzalcoatlus uses his powerful wings
to lift the air conditioners onto the roof.

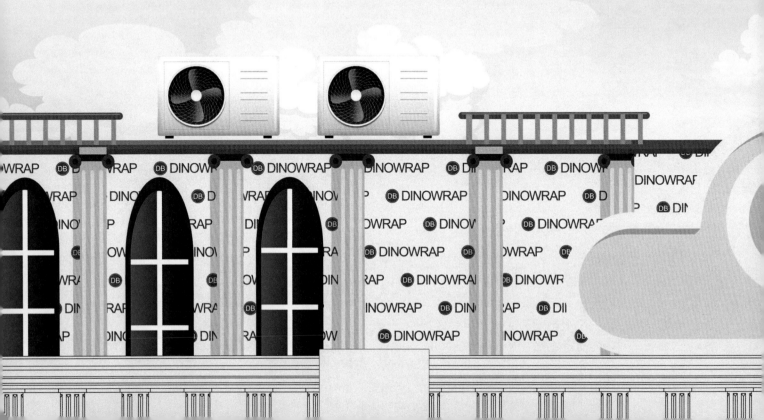

Andy Ankylosaurus and Stacey Stegosaurus use the telescopic forklift to move the pallets of bricks and get the walls built.

Tommy Tyrannosaurus is working hard to get the walls finished up, while Vinney Velociraptor and the gang put in the shiny new floors!

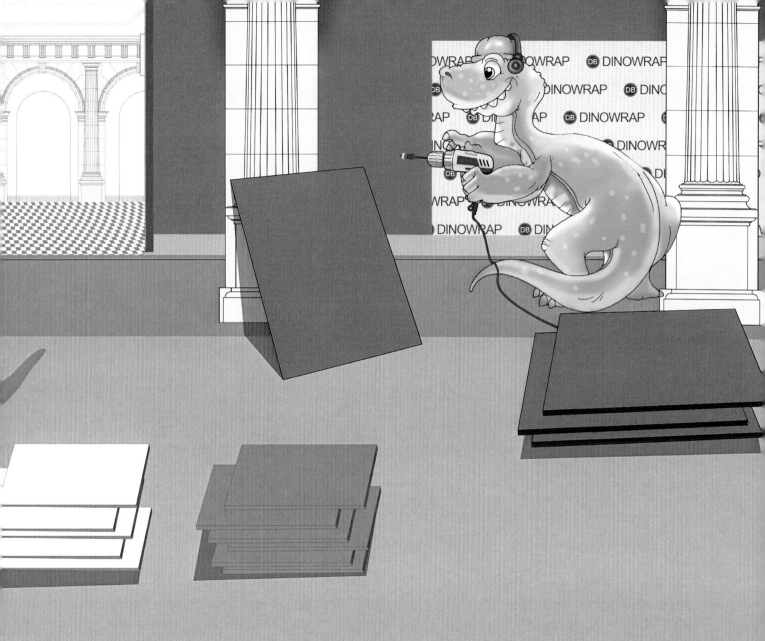

Have you figured out what this building will be?
Soon enough, all will see!

Here comes Billy Baryonyx with the moving truck.

Tammy Triceratops uses the forklift to help bring in all the huge packages!

This Dino Build was a monumental feat,
just a few finishing touches to make it complete!

Patty Parasaurolophus and Scotty Spinosaurus
finish up the landscaping!

Now the building is finished and it is time to clean! The whole Dino Builders team works together to get this last task complete. Now they can celebrate the Grand Opening of the...

Brand new Dino Valley Museum! Great job Dino Builders!

DB DINO-PRONUNCIATION!

Ankylosaurs	ang-ky-lo-saw-ruhs
Baryonyx	bah-ree-on-icks
Brachiosaurus	brae-kee-uh-saw-ruhs
Parasaurolophus	par-ah-sawr-ol-uh-fus
Quetzalcoatlus	ket-suhl-kow-at-luhs
Spinosaurus	spine-oh-saw-ruhs
Stegosaurus	steh-guh-saw-ruhs
Triceratops	trai-seh-ruh-taaps
Tyrannosaurus rex	tr-a-nuh-saw-ruhs rex
Velociraptor	vuh-laa-sr-ap-tr

Made in United States
North Haven, CT
17 February 2022

16193534R00018